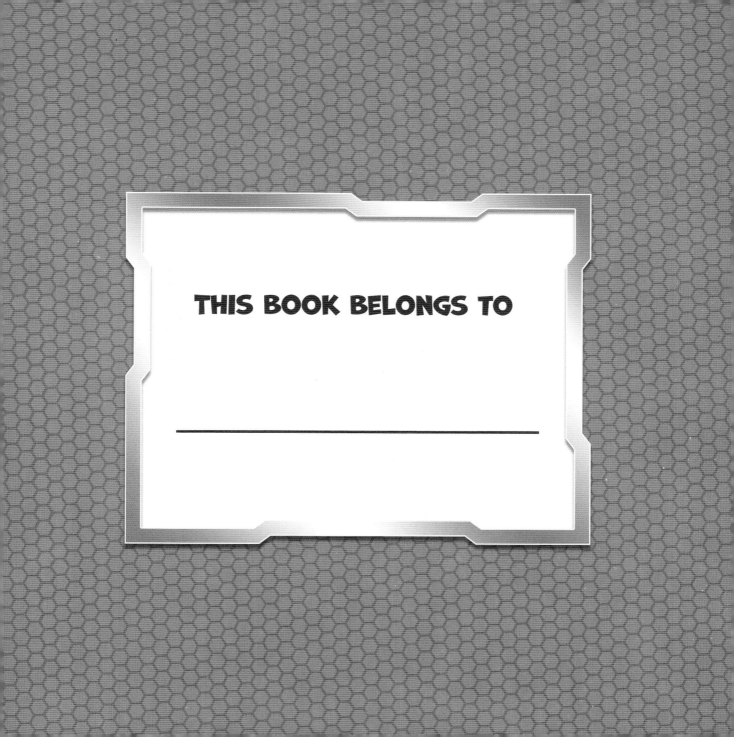

THIS BOOK BELONGS TO

_____

PUPS SAVE RYDER'S ROBOT

ZING!

It was an exciting day at the Lookout. Ryder's new invention, Robo Dog, was complete! He switched it on and the robot barked then rolled forward on his wheeled feet. "Yes," said Ryder, jumping in the air. "Robo Dog is working!"

"Cool robot," said Skye.

Ryder was eager to play with the new pup. "Let's try digging!" Ryder moved the joystick and Robo Dog dug a hole so deep that he soon disappeared.

"Where'd he go?" said Ryder, peering down the hole.

Zuma was asleep in his Pup House when Robo Dog popped up right underneath him! The little robot had dug a tunnel.

"Whoa! Where did you come from?" said Zuma with a laugh.

"Let's try flying," said Ryder.

With the press of a button, Robo Dog's paws turned into jets and he zoomed through the air.

READY...
SET...

GO!

It was time to see how fast the robot could run.

"No robot can outrun me!" said Marshall.

Marshall wanted to race the robot! Chase shouted into his megaphone. "On your bark! Get set! Go!"

I'M OKAY!

They started to race, but just as Marshall took the lead, he tripped and rolled over a fence and into a log.

Robo Dog pushed Marshall out of the log — the race was back on! Then Ryder pushed the Turbo Power button and Robo Dog zoomed ahead!

Just then, Marshall crashed into Ryder and Ryder landed on the robot.

OOF!

"The antenna is bent and broken," said Marshall.

Robo Dog spun in circles, twitching and buzzing. Ryder tried to stop him, but the robot dug a tunnel and disappeared!

Suddenly, Robo Dog appeared on Main Street.

He smashed into Mr. Porter's fruit display. The fruit flew into the air and landed on everyone's head! Then the electric pup knocked Mayor Goodway into the flowers.

Mayor Goodway called Ryder. "Help! Someone's peculiar pet pooch has gone positively punchy!"

Ryder knew the cause of the mechanical mayhem — Robo Dog!

"PAW Patrol to the Lookout!" said Ryder.

The team had to stop the robot before he caused any more problems. But before they could fix Robo Dog, they had to catch Robo Dog!

"Skye, with your goggles, you should be able to locate him. Rocky, I need you to help us build something so we can catch him."

"Let's take to the sky!" said Skye.

"Green means go!" barked Rocky.

The rest of the pups went into town to help clean up all the mess Robo Dog was making.

PUPS AWAY!

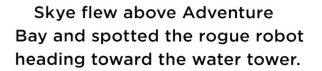

Skye flew above Adventure Bay and spotted the rogue robot heading toward the water tower.

Robo Dog crashed into the water tower, out of the other side, and then flew straight through the wall of Katie's Pet Parlor!

Katie and Cali jumped out of the way . . . and into a bubbly bath!

"Guess he didn't want to use the doggie door," said Katie.

SMASH!

Meanwhile, Rubble and Zuma helped clean up Main Street.

"Thanks for helping, pups!" said Mr. Porter.

Just then, Robo Dog whipped across the sky. He dipped down toward the store and knocked over all the produce . . . again!

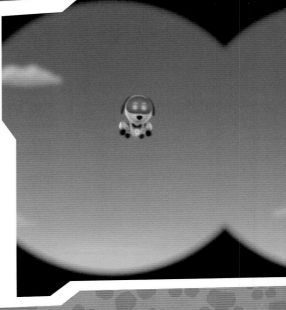

High in the air, Skye spotted something.

"Can you get him to fly toward Rocky's truck?" Ryder asked.

"I'll do my best!" said Skye, swooping away from the runaway robot.

Down below, Rocky was busy making a
contraption to catch the computerized canine. All he
had to do was launch the magnet into the air . . .
then hope it would stick to Robo Dog's metal body!

Skye led Robo Dog closer to Rocky.

Rocky launched the magnet, it flew high into the air, and — THWACK — it stuck to the robot!

WHIZZ!

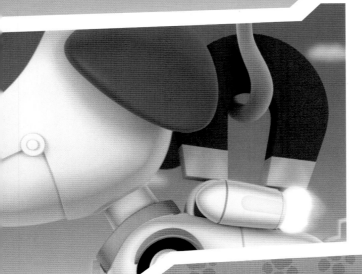

Then it was Skye's turn. She lowered the helicopter's hook and slipped it through the magnet. Hooray! Robo Dog was coming home!

Skye lowered Robo Dog onto Mr. Porter's patio.

"I guess it's back to the drawing board," Ryder said sadly, turning off Robo Dog.

"Hold on, Ryder," said Rocky. "I've got an old antenna. I think it'll work."

Ryder changed the antenna and it worked!

The robot was back to normal. *BARK! BARK!*

"Thanks, Rocky! And thanks to all you pups, too," said Ryder. "I couldn't have fixed him without you!"

"Well, if you're ever in trouble, Ryder . . ." said Rocky. "Just yelp for help!"